Illustrated by

First published in 2014
by Franklin Watts

Cover design by Peter Scoulding

Franklin Watts
338 Euston Road
London NW1 3BH

Franklin Watts Australia
Level 17/207 Kent Street
Sydney, NSW 2000

A CIP catalogue record for this book is available from the British Library.

(pb) ISBN: 978 1 4451 2388 2
(ebook) ISBN: 978 1 4451 2390 5
(Library ebook) ISBN: 978 1 4451 2392 9

1 3 5 7 9 10 8 6 4 2

Printed and bound by CPI Group (UK) Ltd, Croydon, CR0 4YY

Franklin Watts is a division of Hachette Children's Books,
an Hachette UK company.
www.hachette.co.uk

Contents

Chapter One
Top Secret Files

Gestapo offices of German Intelligence, Paris, April 1943.
CLICK
CLICK
There are over forty pages here...
...so little time.
Hell! Spiegel is back from lunch early!
HA-HA-HA!

Very funny! Ha-ha.

Mein gott!

Gack

Crashing into the furniture, British Secret Agent Paul Carter grappled with Hauptmann Spiegel. But Spiegel managed to reach a switch on his desk and smack it with his palm.

Alarm bells rang throughout the building.

Paul summoned his strength, slammed Spiegel against the wall, sunk a clenched fist into the Hauptmann's face and then renewed his grip around his neck. A twist, a snap and the burly Nazi went limp in Paul's grasp. He let the body slide gently to the floor.

Paul lunged for the window and leaped out, grabbing hold of a metal rung on the fire escape's ladder.
He was three floors up with his legs pedalling in the air, his body swinging

precariously. It was too high to jump from, but at any moment he might be spotted and shot. He gained a footing and began clambering down, until he could wait no longer.

Paul let go and dropped into the alley below. He landed, knees bent, and rolled just as he had when parachuting into France a month earlier. Scrambling to his feet, he sprinted along the narrow alleyway. As he approached the street he slowed down to avoid attracting too much attention.

Paul's accomplice, Jacques Dupuis, was waiting across the street by a lamppost as agreed. He was reading a newspaper, trying not to look suspicious.

Jacques had heard the alarm and now saw Paul swiftly heading his way.

He ought to have felt relieved that Paul got out alive, but he didn't. All he felt was dread. It was the look of terror on Paul's face. Paul's work wasn't over yet, either. The handover still needed to be deftly executed, a sleight of hand worthy of any great magician.

Chapter Two
Disaster!

The two men exchanged the faintest of nods as Paul brushed past, slipping the miniature camera into Jacques's pocket.

The street was suddenly alive with soldiers, dozens pouring out of doorways. Jacques sensed their plan unravelling before his eyes. With the camera and its microfilm safely in his pocket, he calmly set off in the opposite direction.

Jacques deliberately ignored the yelling, the orders to "Halt!" bellowed so loud they carried far down the street. He pictured Paul running, arms pumping, and willed him to succeed in

Halt!

getting away. A single shot rang out. A woman screamed. Jacques risked glancing over his shoulder and felt a giddying wave of nausea pass over him. There Paul was, sprawled on the pavement, howling in agony and clutching his leg. In seconds he was surrounded by men in grey uniforms.

Jacques hurried on, his mind ablaze with terrible thoughts. It could so easily have been him. He and Paul had drawn straws for who would raid the Nazis' offices. Now he actually wished Paul was dead, for all their sakes. With Paul arrested, the Germans would interrogate him. Despite their training Jacques knew that most secret agents talked, eventually. Of course Paul would hold out for as long as he could,

tell a few lies, string the Nazis along with some cock-and-bull story littered with false names and addresses that would delay them. In training they'd been told to try to hold out for 48 hours, long enough for others to be warned. Not long, thought Jacques, unless some Gestapo thug is tearing out your toenails, one by one. Then the nightmare would seem never-ending.

Jacques headed for the Metro, taking the first train to a part of Paris called Montmartre, the location of their safe house. Hélène, his radio operator, would be anxiously awaiting their return. She and Paul were close. News of his capture would be devastating, but Jacques knew she was strong. Somehow she'd cope. She had to.

He'd get her to send an urgent coded wireless message to London, explaining that he had the microfilm but that Paul had been arrested. Then, without Paul, they'd head for the French coast as planned. If their dwindling luck held out, they'd soon deliver the microfilm safely to their superiors in London. He prayed that it was all worth it, that his fellow agent's life had not been sacrificed for nothing.

When Jacques reached the busy streets of Montmartre he walked straight to his apartment block. All seemed normal, but as always he glanced up to the fifth-floor window of his flat. He stopped dead the second he spotted it. One curtain was half drawn. It was a signal. Hélène was in trouble too. He dipped into a doorway further along the street and waited. Half an hour passed by. No one went in and no one came out. As best he could tell the building wasn't being watched. He made his move, knocking on a side door that belonged to a ground-floor neighbour, an old lady called Madame Clichet.

As soon as the door opened, Jacques pushed inside.

"Get out!" Madame Clichet hissed.

"Have you seen Hélène?"

"Yes, the Gestapo came and took her away almost two hours ago," the old lady explained, wringing her hands on a cloth, frightened for her life in case anyone had seen Jacques at her door. "They are still up there. I think they are waiting. Now, you must go!

Go!" Madame Clichet pushed Jacques towards the door.

"Your late husband. Do you still have an old coat of his? And an old hat?" He forced a hand against the doorframe. "Please!"

The old lady nodded. "OK, wait there."

Chapter Three
Run, Spy, Run!

Disguised in a dusty old grey raincoat and brown trilby, Jacques left the apartment block behind and walked the streets. He needed time to think. Was he being followed? He had to find out. Zigzagging across the road, he gazed beyond his reflection in shop windows, and doubled back twice. He knelt to tie his shoelaces while glancing behind, and then entered numerous shops. He went in through one door and left by a different exit. Eventually, he decided nobody was tailing him. He was safe – for now. With the evening drawing in and the light fading, Jacques took refuge in a café-bar and ordered a stiff drink. He sat in the corner, behind a screen, away from curious stares. He didn't want anybody asking why he couldn't stop trembling.

Jacques wondered whether it was just bad luck that Paul had been captured and that Hélène had been arrested too. A coincidence? He thought not. The Nazis must've known about their safe house. Worse, they must've known about it even before Paul's capture. They had been betrayed. But by who? Jacques had no idea. He reached into his pocket to check he still had the camera and its microfilm. Perhaps the answer lay in the list of names Paul had photographed. Maybe among the names of informers were fellow members of their

Resistance circuit. Had someone been compromised, threatened, bribed or blackmailed into betraying their fellow agents, or had his circuit been infiltrated by a double agent? Jacques knew his bosses in London feared as much, and that's why they'd sent him to find out. He also realised he could no longer trust any of his contacts. In fact, he couldn't trust anyone at all.

Or could he?

Jacques recalled growing up in the Paris suburbs and the kindly old priest at his local church. Maybe he would offer him shelter – just for a night or two.

At the church, Father Marcel was surprised to see Jacques and, as they embraced, said, "When the authorities decreed that all men aged between 18 and 20 must be transported to Germany to work in the Nazis' factories, I wasn't surprised you disappeared. It's good to see you, Jacques. I won't ask where you've been, but from your manner am I right in thinking you're in trouble?"

Jacques nodded. "Can you hide me? Just for a day or two. Until I can escape."

The interior of the church was lit by hundreds of candles that flickered, casting weird and monstrous shadows. It was dark outside and the curfew less than an hour away. Father Marcel knew that sending the young man back out onto the deserted streets at such a late hour was simply too dangerous. If seen by the police or an army patrol,

Jacques would automatically be arrested. He smiled reassuringly.

"Yes, you can stay. But I do have one question for you. Where do you need to escape to?"

"England. It's my job..."

Father Marcel raised a hand. "Don't utter another word. Even in a house of God sometimes walls have ears."

Jacques wasn't intending to offer any more, although he wished he could have explained that he was an agent, part of Churchill's secret army, that after he'd fled to England he'd been recruited and trained before being sent back to France on a vital mission. A great many lives were at stake and the microfilm in his pocket might hold the answer. His superiors in London could compare the list of names against their own records of agents operating all over northern France. A name appearing on both lists would point to the traitor's identity.

"I may be able to assist you," Father Marcel offered in a clandestine whisper. "I know someone I can trust and who helps people like you. Tomorrow I shall call on him. Come, let me make you something to eat. You look famished. And then you need to get some sleep."

Sleep, thought Jacques, how can I sleep?

Chapter Four
Hear No Evil, See No Evil, Speak No Evil

For two days and nights Jacques hid in the church, the camera practically burning a hole in his pocket. In the end he decided to discard the camera, and sew the microfilm into the lining of his jacket pocket for safekeeping. On the third morning a man in overalls entered the church. He smelled strongly of engine grease. Father Marcel introduced him to Jacques.

"This is Raymond. He works on the railways, but in his spare time he helps people get out of France."

Raymond shook hands firmly with Jacques. "You must come with me now. You will stay at my house until it is time to leave. You will be safe there."

Although fearful at placing his life in the hands of a complete stranger, Jacques knew he had little choice.

Raymond's house was in a street close to the grime and coal dust of the railway yards. Inside, Raymond introduced Jacques to his wife and to another man sitting at the kitchen table. The other man was a British airman called Tommy. He had bailed out when his Halifax bomber was shot down to the south of Paris. Tommy had sprained his ankle on landing, and as a result walked with a limp. He also spoke very little French. Raymond explained that Tommy was going to accompany Jacques during his escape. They weren't heading for the coast,

or to neutral Switzerland, but to the border with Spain.

"You will travel by train," Raymond elaborated. "As far as a small town called Saint-Girons. There you will be met by a guide who will take you over the Pyrenees mountain passes to Spain. After that you're on your own."

"Now, wait a minute. This is madness," Jacques protested. "Tommy can barely walk. Crossing the mountains at this time of year is going to be tough even for the able-bodied."

Raymond's expression hardened. "If Tommy has enough courage, he will find the strength. He understands the risks. He knows that however hard it gets, he must walk or die."

Jacques wasn't done protesting.

"And all that way by train? The Gestapo will check passengers. And he hardly speaks any French! As soon as he opens his mouth we'll both be dead!"

Raymond nodded. "And that's why Father Marcel came up with the perfect cover story. Tommy here is going to pretend to be deaf, dumb and blind. And you are going to be his brother. You are taking him on a pilgrimage to Lourdes where you will both pray for a miracle cure, just like many have done in the past and continue to do so today, despite the war."

Jacques stood up and paced the room. "Madness. It won't work."

"It has to work," an angry Raymond spat back. "We are having all the correct false papers made for him."

Jacques lunged forward and slammed a fist onto the table, making everyone flinch, including Tommy. "See! If he's deaf, how come he heard that? The Germans aren't stupid. If they're even slightly suspicious they'll test him, and he'll fail, and we'll both be done for."

Stirring a pot of potato stew, Raymond's wife interrupted them. "We are risking much in order to help you. I know you understand that. Perhaps in return you can help us. You can speak English. Teach Tommy here to pretend to be deaf, dumb and blind. Help him learn to ignore everything around him, like sudden noises or movements."

Jacques felt like tearing his hair out. "How long have I got?"

"Five days. Maybe less."

Chapter Five
A Lucky Escape

As their crowded train trundled south through mile after mile of wintry countryside, villages and towns, Jacques saw few signs of spring and wished he'd had more time to train the man sitting beside him. Tommy had at least mastered a deadpan expression

and the ability to walk with the fearful uncertainty of someone unable to see where they were going. For five days and nights Jacques had slammed doors, dropped dishes, crept up on Tommy and yelled his name without warning, and for the most part Tommy had learnt to ignore any sudden noise.

There was, however, one major flaw. If Tommy fell asleep, he could still be woken, startled by a noise. Jacques knew the only solution was to keep him awake, at all times, prodding him if his head dropped. It meant Jacques had to stay awake too.

The train stopped in Toulouse. Jacques guided his "brother" onto the platform and left him sitting on a bench for a moment while he sought information on their connection to Saint-Girons at the ticket office. He returned to find a man in a dark leather raincoat staring curiously at Tommy.

The Gestapo! Jacques was sure of it.

Before Jacques could reach his travelling companion, the Nazi had begun questioning Tommy and reacted angrily when it appeared that the man on the bench was ignoring every word. Ignoring the Gestapo was extremely unwise. Tommy just sat motionless, his expression blank, as the Nazi began shouting, demanding to see his papers, demanding answers.

"Can't you see he's deaf and blind?" Jacques called out, hurrying to intervene. "He's mute too. Here, let me get his papers for you." Jacques reached inside the pocket of Tommy's coat. "There, you will see everything is in order."

The Gestapo snatched the papers and

studied them carefully.

"I'm taking him to Lourdes, to pray for a miracle cure," Jacques added, predicting the Nazi's next question. He handed over his papers for inspection too. The seconds ticked by. They

turned into minutes. The man from the Gestapo stared first at Tommy and then Jacques, his expression at best doubting, at worst highly suspicious. Then he handed the papers back, turned on his heel and walked away.

Jacques seized Tommy's arm and got him to his feet. "Come on, we've got another train to catch," he whispered. "That was too close for comfort."

They'd walked barely twenty yards when a shot rang out. Jacques instinctively crouched down. He glanced round and saw that the Gestapo had ordered a soldier to fire his rifle into the air. Their deception was being tested. Then Jacques realised Tommy had remained standing, unmoved, perfectly still, seemingly

oblivious to the shot. It was enough to satisfy the Nazi. Jacques rose to his feet, grabbed Tommy's arm once more and hurried on. "I must have trained you better than I'd thought," he whispered.

"I expected something like that," Tommy whispered back. "I heard a rifle bolt being slid back and forth. Call it a lucky escape."

Chapter Six
Leap of Faith

As dusk fell and the chugging steam locomotive pulled the string of carriages towards Saint-Girons and the foothills and mountains beyond, Jacques began to relax a little. Their carriage was only a third full and not a soldier in sight. The conductor worked his way along the rows, checking tickets and leaning across to pull down the window blinds. When he reached Jacques and Tommy he whispered, "The station at Saint-Girons isn't safe. They are checking everyone thoroughly. But don't worry, you are among friends. In about ten minutes we shall slow down. Make your way to the rear door.

The driver will blow the whistle when the time comes."

"Time for what?" asked Jacques.

"To jump, of course. Your guide awaits you."

Jacques felt gripped by a cold numbness. The plan had changed. That was never a good sign. But they had little choice. He waited five minutes and then guided Tommy to the rear of the last carriage. "You can ditch the disguise for now. Are you ready?"

Tommy nodded. "Is there a good way of doing this?"

Jacques recalled his training carried out in the Scottish Highlands under the watchful eye of a bullish sergeant major. "Yes. Crouch down on the footplate, let go and roll as best you can."

WOoooOW!
CHUFF
CHUFF

Ooof!

You OK?
Yes, just my damn leg complaining.

Chapter Seven
A Man of Few Words

A flash of torchlight in their faces, the briefest of handshakes, and the command “Follow me” were their only introduction to their guide. Alain was a shepherd turned Resistance fighter turned mountain guide. He knew the upper slopes of the hills where he tended his animals like the back of his hand. He trudged off, rifle slung over his shoulder. Alain was a man of few words.

Through the darkness they crossed roads, climbed fences, silently crept past farm buildings and entered a narrow trail leading into a forest. Their ascent steepened and soon Tommy was struggling. Jacques lent a hand, but still their progress proved slow. Alain eventually paused long enough to curse them.

"Can we stop a minute? Tommy here needs to catch his breath."

Alain trudged back to where they stood and shoved his face up close to Jacques. "*Non!* We walk. We keep moving. The Germans have doubled their patrols. They are out every night. And we are late. The others will be waiting. If we stop they might go on without us."

"I'm fine, let's carry on," Tommy replied, reckoning he'd understood the gist of what they'd said in French.

In silence they walked on, up and beyond the forest, across boulder-strewn icy fields, the night air freezing their laboured breath. Jacques had not questioned what Alain had meant about the "others", but as they approached an old stone barn shrouded in trees, he guessed others would be joining them in their bid for freedom. And entering the barn, his heart sank. A dozen frightened figures: some elderly, some clearly half-starved, a child no more than eight years old. Jacques feared none had the strength for the climb ahead of them. In the corner sat a second guide, Alain's brother, Marc.

Marc struck Jacques as edgy. He seemed keen to leave at once. There was much he wanted to whisper into Alain's ear while making gestures that hinted of trouble. Tommy briefly sat

down on a bale of straw shivering and rubbing his hands together. Then he got back up. "I need a leak," he announced to Jacques. "I'm going outside."

Still observing the animated discussion between their guides, Jacques responded, "Good idea. I need a leak too."

Chapter Eight
By the Skin of Their Teeth

They walked just a few dozen yards from the barn and relieved themselves in the midst of the trees and bushes.

"Something's not right," Jacques remarked.

"Did you catch what they were talking about?"

"Only snatches. Something about people being arrested and rounded up. It seems we've come at a particularly dangerous time."

A noise. A flash of light.

"Jesus, get down! Germans!"

Crouching and staring into the darkness they began to see shapes, shapes of men moving, a dozen of them at least.

BANG!
BANG!
BANG!

Jacques and Tommy watched the prisoners being led away.

"Guess that's it then," Tommy stuttered. "No guide, no one to show us the way. We're done for."

Jacques gazed at the barn. How ironic, he thought, that they too must've had traitors in their midst. He shook himself free of such dark thoughts. He recalled his agent's survival training, although he reckoned it hardly prepared him for the task facing them now. To survive they needed a plan. They needed to find shelter, somewhere safe, if there was such a place. Then they'd head west, towards Spain, trusting their instincts, hoping they chose the right trails and paths, praying they'd not bump into enemy patrols. Then he felt overwhelmed at the thought of snow-covered mountain trails fit only for goats, biting winds that could knock a man off his feet, frostbite that could eat through fingers and toes, and the ever-present fear of death.

"Follow me. Do not make a sound."

Startled, Jacques snapped his head round and saw Alain standing right behind him. "B—b—but..."

"I also needed to take a...leak," he replied.

"And your brother, Marc?"

"You heard the shots as well as I did." The bitterness in Alain's voice was unmistakable. "He's dead."

"Do you know who betrayed you?"

Alain dropped his head and spat at

the ground. "No, not yet. But when I return I shall find out and they will pay the price. Now, we must move. It isn't safe here and we've a long way to go."

Jacques rose to his feet and spotted something in Alain's expression that chilled him to the bone. It was a look full of suspicion and distrust. And then Jacques understood. How convenient it must seem that he and Tommy had left the barn just in time to escape the Germans. It was pure coincidence, but Alain wasn't to know that. Jacques decided to say nothing more and instead helped Tommy to his feet. "Best we keep a close eye on our guide. I'm not sure he trusts us, Tommy. And if he thinks we had a hand in all this, we're dead men."

Chapter Nine
Mountain High, River Deep

A night spent huddled in the sheltered crack between two enormous granite boulders left Jacques with a stiff back and Tommy barely able to walk. Alain stood before them in the heavy mist, scowling and cursing.

"We must climb today." Alain pointed to the west. "To over 2,600 metres. Is your friend up to it? If not, we leave him here."

"He'll make it," Jacques replied. "Even if I have to carry him."

Alain nodded. "You may have to."

They climbed through snowfields and jumbles of slippery boulders that on first inspection seemed to offer no manageable route. Alain moved sure-footedly, each step considered, his pace constant, grinding down Jacques's and Tommy's dwindling strength. Frequent stops were necessary. Jacques gasped the thinning air and felt his sweat freeze beneath his shirt. Alain just gazed at them pitifully before heading on, cursing that he'd been lumbered with such feeble men.

Slowly the mist cleared, bringing the mountains into full view. Deep valleys revealed fast-flowing rivers at their bottom, edged by snow-covered scree slopes and clumps of forest. Above towered the peaks of the Pyrenees. A beautiful sight, Jacques thought, so long as you didn't have to climb them, which is exactly what fate awaited

them. Up and up they climbed, Alain following trails that were to Jacques invisible, lost beneath the knee-deep snow. Then along narrow ledges, one step at a time, clinging onto walls of rock so cold that it felt as though his hands were burning. Then more snowfields, a grinding, sapping trudge that seemed unending.

Bent double, heaving for breath, Tommy had gone about as far as he could. Alain stopped and let the small rucksack he was carrying slip from his back. “We stop to eat here. Ten minutes and then we carry on.” He undid the straps of his rucksack and produced small loaves of bread which he handed out along with chunks of cooked meat.

“How far now?” Jacques asked. “Can we see the border from here?”

Alain shook his head.

Huddled and shivering uncontrollably, Tommy looked increasingly unwell, pale and in great discomfort. Jacques nevertheless had a growing admiration for the young airman. Not once in all the time they'd been together had he complained or admitted to being scared. Jacques supposed that if it was him unable to speak the language, barely able to walk, and having to rely on complete strangers to guide him to safety on a dangerous journey, he'd be pretty scared too. He resolved that whatever it took, Tommy deserved to succeed.

Without warning Alain leaped to his feet, shielded his eyes and scanned the sky.

"What's the matter?"

Squinting, Alain continued to gaze up, tracking slowly along the mountain peaks and ridges.

Up there!

Quick! Hide!

Do you think it's seen us?
Who knows? Guess we'll soon find out.

A sharp descent was followed by another lung-bursting climb. As daylight faded Alain declared they'd gone far enough for one day. To cheer his travellers he pointed and said, "Tomorrow you go down, and there you will find Spain!"

Chapter Ten
Abandoned

Falling into a deep sleep, Jacques awoke at first light to find that Alain had gone. Struck with panic he leaped awkwardly to his feet and roused Tommy.

"Gone? What do you mean gone? Have we been betrayed?"

It was a question Jacques couldn't answer. "Come on, we head west, just as Alain said. Let's pray to God he's not delivered us into the arms of the enemy."

So they set off alone, uncertain and fearful. Jacques reckoned there could be only two explanations for Alain vanishing without a word. Either they'd been left to suffer a dreadful fate or they were sufficiently close to the border to be able to find their own way. He also suspected Alain was desperate to return home, to discover who'd betrayed him and his brother, the fire of revenge burning in his belly. Jacques reached deep into an inside pocket and felt for the hidden microfilm, sewn into the lining for safekeeping. Looking back in the direction of Saint-Girons, he wished Alain good hunting. Then he grabbed Tommy's arm and shouldered him on along the snow-covered path, both desperately battling against a biting wind.

An hour later they were descending and with each step their optimism grew. Mid-afternoon they came across a sign.

At the end of their tether they just stood and stared at it. Jacques began to laugh uncontrollably.

"What does it say?" Tommy asked, letting go of Jacques and sinking to his knees.

"God knows, Tommy," Jacques replied. "It's in Spanish."

Author's Note

During the Second World War many escape lines were established out of Nazi-occupied France. Their success was solely due to the extraordinary courage of many ordinary men and women who risked their own lives by hiding escapees, feeding and clothing them, and acting as their chaperones and guides on arduous and dangerous journeys. Many were caught and suffered the terrible consequences. There were numerous escape routes across the mountains of the Pyrenees including several starting from Saint-Girons. Today, it is still possible to walk and climb one of them in what is now known as "The Freedom Trail", the route being marked for those with the courage and stamina to attempt it.

This story was inspired by events that happened in several real and successful escapes.

WORLD WAR SHORT STORIES

There are four books to collect!

978 1 4451 2382 0 pb 978 1 4451 2384 4 ebook

978 1 4451 2381 3 pb 978 1 4451 2383 7 ebook

978 1 4451 2388 2 pb 978 1 4451 2390 5 ebook

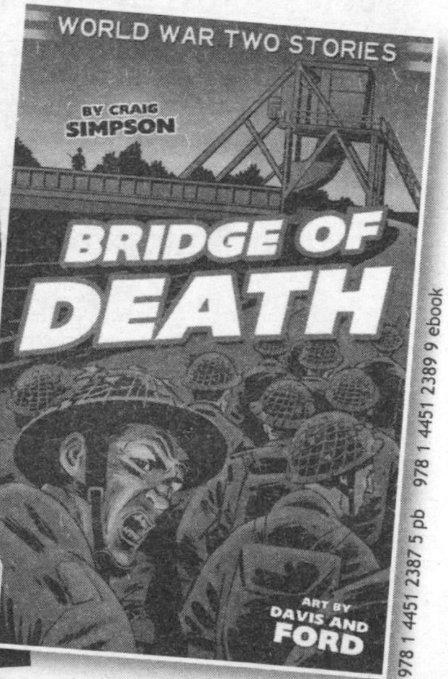

978 1 4451 2387 5 pb 978 1 4451 2389 9 ebook